IMPOSSIBLE
MOON

FOR GRANA, WHO GOT ME TO
THE MOON LOTS OF TIMES AND
WAS ALWAYS THERE TO WELCOME
ME BACK—B. J. M.

TO MY MOTHER, SHERRY.
THANK YOU FOR ALWAYS
SHOWING ME TO DREAM BIG,
REACH FOR THE STARS, AND
REMEMBER TO BREATHE—T. E.

SIMON & SCHUSTER BOOKS FOR YOUNG READERS
An imprint of Simon & Schuster Children's Publishing Division
1230 Avenue of the Americas, New York, New York 10020
Text © 2022 by Breanna McDaniel
Illustration © 2022 by Tonya Engel
Book design by Lucy Ruth Cummins © 2022 by Simon & Schuster, Inc.
SIMON & SCHUSTER BOOKS FOR YOUNG READERS and related marks are
trademarks of Simon & Schuster, Inc.
For information about special discounts for bulk purchases, please contact Simon & Schuster
Special Sales at 1-866-506-1949 or business@simonandschuster.com.
The Simon & Schuster Speakers Bureau can bring authors to your live event. For more
information or to book an event, contact the Simon & Schuster Speakers Bureau
at 1-866-248-3049 or visit our website at www.simonspeakers.com.
The text for this book was set in Horley Old Style.
The illustrations for this book were rendered in oil over acrylic under-painting on bristol paper.
Manufactured in China
0322 SCP
First Edition
10 9 8 7 6 5 4 3 2 1
Library of Congress Cataloging-in-Publication Data
Names: McDaniel, Breanna J., author. | Engel, Tonya, illustrator.
Title: Impossible moon / Breanna McDaniel ; illustrated by Tonya Engle.
Description: First edition. | New York : Simon & Schuster Books for Young Readers, 2022. |
Audience: Ages 4–8. | Audience: Grades K–1. | Summary: Mable goes on an impossible
quest to the moon hoping that will cure her beloved Grana, and is aided by constellations
associated with African and African American history along the way. Includes brief
descriptions of the constellations mentioned, and a note on the myth or history associated
with each.
Identifiers: LCCN 2020050229 (print) | LCCN 2020050230 (ebook) |
ISBN 9781534478978 (hardcover) | ISBN 9781534478985 (ebook)
Subjects: CYAC: Voyages, Imaginary—Fiction. | Constellations—Fiction. | Folklore,
Africa—Fiction. | African Americans—Fiction. | Sick—Fiction. | Grandmothers—Fiction.
Classification: LCC PZ7.1.M43432 Imp 2022 (print) | LCC PZ7.1.M43432 (ebook) |
DDC [E]—dc23
LC record available at https://lccn.loc.gov/2020050229
LC ebook record available at https://lccn.loc.gov/2020050230

IMPOSSIBLE MOON

words by BREANNA J. MCDANIEL   pictures by TONYA ENGEL

A DENENE MILLNER BOOK
Simon & Schuster Books for Young Readers
New York London Toronto Sydney New Delhi

When Grana was better,
she told Mable the best stories.

Nowadays, Grana lies in bed.
Still smiling.
Still creaky and wrinkly and warm.
She's too weak to tell stories now.
It seems impossible she'll ever
get better.
But her stories beat strong in
Mable's heart, and for now,
Grana is still here.

Mable stays close, mapping constellations and listening,
just in case Grana has a little story to share.
    One day Grana points to Mable's moon maps and
says, "If we can touch the moon,
then what is impossible?"

Later, at bedtime, Mable's gaze lands on the moon.
Its light, bright and magnificent, calls her to it.

Mable's bed becomes a trampoline,
her bedsheets wings,
and she bets she can bounce to the moon.
She bets she can make impossible things possible.

Mable counts down, then jets through the window, up, up, and away.

She spies a drinking gourd,
and stops for a sip.
     As Mable cups sky water from the dipper,
she looks way down to the ground
and sees crisscrossing tracks.

She imagines they are a long-ago
railroad that people rode to freedom.

She doesn't see the lion slowly
creeping up behind her
Until . . . he growls . . .
real soft.

She whispers, "Courage, Mable."
Knees knocking, wings quivering,
she inhales and . . .

Mable is saved by
a shooting star!
Suddenly the king is a kitten,
off to capture the light.

Heart pounding,
wings beating,

Mable
swivels in
the air and . . .

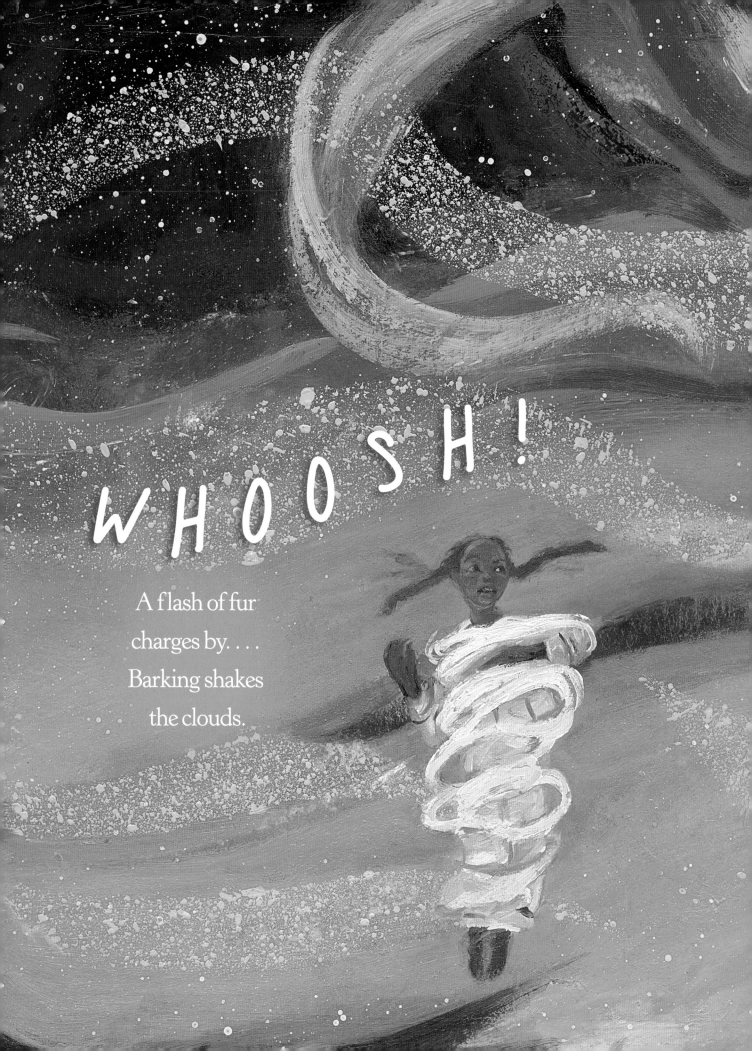

WHOOSH!

A flash of fur
charges by. . . .
Barking shakes
the clouds.

WHOOSH!

Mable struggles through the
thunder and dodges lightning.
The dog's bark is close,
and now the moon is hidden.

Once more she says,
"C'mon! Courage, Mable!" Then she
says in a big voice like her momma's,

"SIT!"

It's still mighty cloudy, but the
storm calms,
and the dog . . .
he sits.

With soft pats to his
neck, Mable asks,
"Who's a good boy?"
She climbs aboard
and says,
"Take me to the
moon, please."

Bounding through
the skies, they pass
twins skipping
through the heavens . . .

and a man pouring out rainwater from a pitcher,
who waves as they fly by.

Then a high-pitched whistle
breaks through the air.
The dog raises his head,
and bounces back toward a man
with a bow and arrow.
Away from the moon.

Mable releases the dog
as the man bends to greet his friend.

She needs to get to the moon
and then back to Grana.

Wait.

Maybe the archer knows where the moon is!

"'Scuse me, sir, I'm on my way to the moon.

Can you tell me which way to go?"

"Up," he says.

Above their heads, there is the moon.
Not close, but not impossible anymore.

The moon shines and an idea bursts
into Mable's mind. "Sir," she says, "a
little help, please?"

Up Mable goes in his palm,
his arm stretching his bow.
Mable is the arrow
shooting straight and true to the moon.
She reaches out her hand to touch
its bright surface,
ready to prove to folks and to herself,
that nothing is impossible. . . .

But Mable misses.

She misses the moon.

Dear Mable,
she's so tired,
and she drifts through the sky,
eyes closed, heart heavy.
        Then . . .
            someone plucks Mable from her fall
        and holds her close.

It's a sistah!

"We got you," the sistah says simply.
Mable is wrapped in a blanket of stars.
Seven times she is passed to loving arms,
each sistah cradling her and sharing
lullabies of
"We got you" and
"Hush, now" and
"Breathe, baby."
Mable is safe, rockabying in
the sky. She yawns and stretches
her hands up, cupping the now
faraway moon in her palm.

She sleeps.

When Mable wakes up, the sun is high.
She rushes to tell Grana about her
journey to touch the moon.
Grana sits up
in her bed.

Impossible before, but now . . .
she's there,
creaky and wrinkly and warm,
saying, "Mable, you tell the
best stories."

Later that night Mable bounces on her bed,
ready to take flight.
Her mission is clear.
Impossible moon?

No such thing.

AUTHOR'S NOTE

A few years ago, I sat on a low stone wall outside a farmhouse in Glasgow, Scotland, exhilarated from an evening of eating, laughing, and traditional Scottish dancing at a *ceilidh* (pronounced kay-lee). I'd traveled to Scotland alone after spending the prior year and a half in Atlanta, Georgia, living with and helping care for my Grana as her health declined. I took this trip to reflect on her life and my own because my heart was starting to understand that her illness was never going to go away. That was hard.

The moon that evening was so close it seemed that if I reached up, I could cup it in my hands. I knew that was impossible, but I reached up my hands anyway and gazed at how the moon sat perfectly in my palms. I pretended to stop time with this moon I was holding in Scotland, knowing it was the same moon rising in Atlanta with my Grana. Eventually I released the moon and went back inside. I think I also released myself to time moving forward, and my Grana, too.

Later, a story began to take shape in my heart. In it, a little girl named Mable who loves the moon and the stars figures that if she can achieve the impossible feat of touching the moon, maybe, just maybe, she can heal her sick grandma. That's a big dream for a little heroine, so I wanted her to have a little help on the way, and so I invited the constellations into my story.

I went to planetariums around the United States to see how they presented stories told about the stars for millennia. I was surprised to see that in planetarium films and slides, Cassiopeia, an Ethiopian queen who angers the Greek god Poseidon by boasting about her daughter's beauty, was often pictured as a White woman with flowing, blond locks. I was disappointed, too, that presentations about the Big Dipper never mentioned the importance of the North Star to enslaved people, who read the night skies to find their way to freedom.

During my visits to planetariums, I also noticed that I was often one of the few Black people present, and that made me worry that Mable's story wouldn't reach Black kids like my nieces and nephews.

Then the film *Black Panther* came out and we saw a princess named Shuri show the world what Black scientists can look like! The gorgeous black-purples of Wakanda's ancestral plain inspired me to explore the constellations in a new way. Although my early vision of a Cassiopeia with a Fro like Pam Grier didn't make it into the final draft of the book, a drinking gourd with a North Star shining above an Underground Railroad did. Pastoral images of joyous Black twins and an archer with long locs did, too. The importance of a community that will literally carry you when you are down-and-out made it to this final draft.

These stories arose from the images of the stars that Mable and other children might see through a telescope or imagine touching as they watch scenes of shuttles launching astronauts into outer space, with grandparents and other loved ones encouraging a love of science and space and story. *Impossible Moon* is also about how reaching for what others say is impossible is sometimes the best way to grow and heal as we push past limitations imposed on our dreams.

THE *IMPOSSIBLE* MOON SKY

An astronomer is a person who studies not just the stars we see but all the different parts of the universe: the planets, galaxies, moons, and comets. Mable's moon maps are one way that she learns about her favorite celestial body. Interested in learning more about moons maps? The National Aeronautics and Space Administration (NASA) has some pretty cool ones on their website.

Constellations are patterns of stars that form shapes in the sky. They help Mable during her journey just like they do for people across the globe who look to them for guidance on when to plant and harvest their crops and celebrate new beginnings and endings. Knowledge and oral stories about constellations are passed down from one generation to the next.

I've learned some of those stories and they have rocketed into this book like shooting stars. Here are some of the stories along with the constellations they are connected to.

THE BIG DIPPER

Enslaved people escaping from the brutality of chattel slavery in the American South were told to follow "the drinking gourd" and use the North Star as a compass to help them to freedom. I always thought the North Star was part of the Big Dipper, but it's actually on the handle of the Little Dipper, a little ways across the sky. Also, the Big Dipper is actually an asterism, or a group of stars not formally recognized as a constellation.

LEO

This mighty constellation is shaped like a lion and is one of the easiest to spot in the night sky, particularly during the spring equinox, when it is most visible. It has always reminded me of the fable of a king whose ego gets humbled, as retold by historian and author Virginia Hamilton in her story "He Lion, Bruh Bear, and Bruh Rabbit." This trickster tale, shared among enslaved folks in the American South, descended from folktales from Indigenous people in western, central, and southern countries in the continent of Africa.

CANIS MAJOR

This constellation's Latin name means "the greater dog" in English. Faithful and always following the Hunter Orion, it made sense for there to be a huge "outside dog" in this community of constellations that has a bark that shakes the heavens but is actually friendlier than anyone could have thought.

AQUARIUS

This constellation, called "the Water Bearer," is one of the oldest documented. It felt important to include Aquarius not because of the Greek myths most associated with it but because I've been taught that water can provide healing and nourishment. Water is precious but not a guarantee for many people around the world. I also wanted to reflect on the transatlantic crossing where so many Black lives were lost during the Middle Passage, covered by the waters but not forgotten.

GEMINI

This constellation is famously known as "the Twins." Here, they represent the double-consciousness of Black folks who live in the United States. We're often determined even when we face the darkest of times, seeking and celebrating joy and care.

ORION

For this constellation, known as "the Hunter," I turned to a Namaqua Khoikhoi myth from what is now known as Namibia to help Mable shoot for the moon. The fable tells of a man who, sent by his wives to hunt, takes only one arrow with him. He shoots the arrow at three zebras—represented by the stars on what is also known as Orion's belt—and misses his prey! Mable shoots straight but still misses . . . the first time.

THE PLEIADES

The Pleiades, known as "Seven Sisters," is a cluster of more than eight hundred stars that look like a smaller version of the Big Dipper. Here, "the Seven Sistahs" represent renewal, as they signal the new year on the Xhosa calendar. The sistahs in the book help Mable find new purpose since they don't let her fall or fail; they just give her what so many of us need to be revived: rest.